Nights in Punktown

A Trio of Dark Science Fiction Stories

JEFFREY THOMAS

The Jeffrey Thomas Chapbook Series

#2

JEFFREY THOMAS

Copyright © 2019 Jeffrey Thomas

All rights reserved.

Cover art by Tithi Luadthong/Shutterstock.com.

This book is a work of fiction. Names, characters, places and incidents are either a product of the author's imagination or are used fictitiously. Any resemblance to actual events, locales or persons, living or dead, is entirely coincidental.

PUBLICATION HISTORY

Draped in Flesh is original to this collection.

Out of Nothing first appeared in the online publication *DarkFuse Magazine*, 2017.

Little Wing first appeared in the publication *Dark Discoveries*, JournalStone, 2018.

CONTENTS

1. DRAPED IN FLESH

2. OUT OF NOTHING

3. LITTLE WING

4. *About the Author*

DRAPED IN FLESH

Isabella didn't know if any of the other tenants had yet ventured to the roof to have a closer look at the mass that had fallen there from the sky.

She herself had only been to the roof on one previous occasion. Last summer, a short time after having moved into this apartment building called Benevento Arms, she had taken her old classmate Clara – visiting from Miniosis, Paxton's larger but less colorful sister city – up to the roof so they could look out at Punktown (as Paxton was more colloquially known) and share a bottle of wine. When they'd stepped out of the little shed that enclosed the stairwell, the two young women had encountered three men about their own age, of Earth heritage like themselves, reclining in foldout lawn chairs with bottles of Zub in hand, staring up at the sky, its underbelly of cloud aglow with neon and laser and holographic advertisements so that it seemed as though they were awaiting the arrival of some prophesized storm of falling colored light. When the men spotted the women, they sat up as if suddenly sober and called for them to join them. The women had begun to retreat back into the graffiti-layered shed, Isabella pulling at her friend's arm.

"Hey," one of the men had called, rising a bit unsteadily to his feet. He was muscular, wearing a white undershirt and shorts, his short hair and thick beard black. "Don't be afraid, ladies! You...you're on floor 8, right? I'm Emir – I'm on 9. Hey, come on, come back! We have a cooler here for your wine!" He gestured. But Isabella had begged off, and Emir and his two similarly built friends had moaned, "Aww!"

In the stairwell, as the door had slid shut, Clara had laughed in a whisper, "Horny fucks."

"Really," Isabella had said, less amused, because she had to live in this building. "They might have tried to get us drunk and rape us."

"Dearie, you're the Punktowner, not me. You know there are a lot worse things in this city than those little boys."

"You don't know that. You never know what someone is capable of," Isabella had replied. "We don't even know what *we're* capable of."

"Anyway," Clara had said, "they weren't cute."

This afternoon, when the door slid back and Isabella stepped out onto the roof, she gratefully found herself alone. Except for the great mass of flesh.

It was winter, the air a rush of knives, but at least it hadn't snowed for a while. Usually Weather Control disallowed that stuff after Christmas.

The air was almost painfully clear to the eye and Punktown stretched off in every direction, first and foremost. Punktown took a backseat to nothing. Since quaint old Benevento Arms had only twelve stories, other buildings soared up past it on all sides, some of them seemingly unto infinity; skyscrapers penetrating the heavens, their upper portions lost in haze. Down below, slow hovercars clotted the streets. Up here, helicars swarmed a bit more freely between the gargantuan columns, like intent hornets.

A massive free-floating hologram advertising some melodramatic VT series, in the Korean language, faced Isabella. Momentarily she stood in place to watch the trailer. She determined the story centered around a love triangle. Lots of soundless yelling and sobbing, even a fistfight between two jealous young men as handsome as models. A gorgeous young woman spat blood into a handkerchief...*uh-oh*. Dramatic terminal illness. Isabella hated love stories. Insipid. They only reminded her of her own love stories, failures like canceled VT shows.

Finally taking her eyes from the holographic trailer, Isabella moved forward upon the rooftop.

The great mass, an airless and collapsed zeppelin of flesh, had come to rest here like a parachute. It covered about three quarters of the roof's surface. Isabella stole upon it warily, as if the massive thing might suddenly shudder, judder, back into life. After all, who could say this glob was actually dead?

It appeared gelatinous, a material that subtly glowed – in a golden metallic way – from within. Tiny bubbles floated slowly, ponderously, through its substance as though through an intoxicating beverage. Isabella knelt at its edge, in awe, to run her hand over this matter as if in a sensuous caress. She found that it wasn't as gelatinous as she had taken it to be, but firmer, almost like soft rubber.

At her approach, a flock of gray birds with tapir-like snouts had shot up from where they had been perched upon the tallest hump of the uneven, protoplasmic mass. Isabella lifted her head to watch them scatter. They hadn't been feeding on the thing, had they? She didn't know these nuisance city birds to be that kind of scavenger. She saw three bird had stayed behind, fluttering their wings madly. It was odd, but their lower bodies seemed partly sunken into the matter. Were they stuck? It wasn't trying to feed on *them*, was it? But after all three of them – more or less at once – gave a strange spasm, the straggler birds launched into the sky, wildly and awkwardly at first, then regained their composure and swept off to catch up with their tribe.

Isabella rose to her feet. She wanted to go to the far side of the building and look down. There, the rubbery golden mass was draped in such a way that it hung down about halfway to the street, obscuring the windows on that side of the building from floors 12 to 7. She knew all too well, because her bedroom window was currently blocked by the thing as though a heavy shade had been drawn to cut off the light. She didn't approach that side of the roof, however, as it would mean actually climbing up onto the blob and walking across it.

She didn't trust it because she didn't know enough about the material's properties, its potential threats, because it hadn't been sufficiently explained to the tenants what the thing was. The landlord had assured them all, in a message sent to their wrist comps, that the Health Agency of Paxton had been notified. HAP had told the landlord that the thing was a portion sloughed off a damaged ship – of "partly organic composition" – coming into Punktown for an emergency landing. The ship itself had landed more or less successfully, with apparently no casualties to either its crew or Punktown citizens. Isabella couldn't recall what race the ship had belonged to, if the landlord had mentioned it at all. There were too many to keep track of in Punktown.

Well, it had been three days now, and no health agents had as yet come to examine the debris, let alone clear it away – however they intended to do that.

The landlord had informed them in a follow-up message, no doubt in response to concerned calls, that the Health Agency hadn't forgotten them...they simply had quite a backlog of work to deal with. This was, after all, Punktown.

Isabella walked along the edge of the thing, where it thinned to a membrane only about two inches in height, as if skirting a surf lest it wet her sneakers. Behind the shed that contained the stairwell – and the mass was partly flopped across its roof – there was a pronounced heap, and upon it she encountered a strange feature that caused her to stop in her tracks.

Here, the golden tissues appeared to had been torn away, or melted bloodlessly away, revealing an isolated bit of interior structure, like a fragment from a titanic skeleton. However, this uncovered object appeared metallic, the color of brass. Was this, then, not part of the "organic" component of the alleged ship?

Weirdly, this structure, consisting mostly of two ring-like shapes – large enough that she could have slipped her body through them – looked to Isabella like a partly exposed set of brass knuckles made for a violent god. She stared up at them, atop their heap, and realized the air within the rings was blurry. Not only blurry, but swirling. Clockwise within one ring, counterclockwise in the other ring.

She grew dizzy staring into them both simultaneously. A strange thought came to her...that this arrangement was a kind of brain, if only a primitive one, perhaps a brain for just this section of the living ship. That data...or calculations...or *thoughts*...swirled around and around in one ring, until they were churned into the proper state to be transferred to the adjacent ring, where they were further processed, or put into usage.

She felt an urge, then, to climb up onto that mound, and thrust her arms into the rings...one in each. This sensation was almost a compulsion. It was as though something – the thoughts whirling in opposite directions around and around in those rings? – was coaxing her. Almost beseeching her, like a melancholy lover that *needed* her.

It needs to rejoin its ship, Isabella thought. This thought seemed more than an intuition to her. It was more a certainty, as though transmitted to her. *It's in pain. It's lonely.*

She tore herself backwards a step. She almost lost her footing...she feared she might black out. She squeezed her eyes shut, squeezed her brain shut, spun away and groped her way back toward the shed in the center of the flat roof.

Isabella got herself inside, slid the door shut behind her. It seemed to cut off the spell. She leaned against the inner wall for a few moments, catching her breath, before she descended back into Benevento Arms.

***

Tomorrow was Valentine's Day. Isabella had almost forgotten, but she received a message from her ex-boyfriend Claudio on her wrist comp and when she opened it, a holographic heart flashed up into the air in front of her, revolving and spewing gold glitter that flickered and fell. It was like some startling booby-trap. Isabella wondered, had he sent this same valentine to the girl he'd been fucking behind her back for over six months before she'd found out? She trashed the message.

What a gruesome holiday, she thought. How grotesque, these old holidays, like Christmas...celebrating the birth of a man who was tortured to death, whose torture was blithely displayed on necklaces and in churches to subdue worshippers with guilt. This St. Valentine, he'd been beheaded – so go eat some chocolates! These cute red hearts exchanged by lovers...they were a crude representation of an organ the size of two clenched fists that pushed blood through the body. Why not revere a liver, instead? The bowels? Hell, what about the brain? A penis, a vagina? Who were they kidding...of course those two bits were what it really boiled down to.

Love, Isabella sneered, if thoughts could sneer. It was just peacock feathers and mating dances. Just the biological impulse to seek a temporary union, an illusion of wholeness, in order to propagate one's species. In the end, about as romantic a function as shitting, wasn't it?

Whatever day it was on Earth that the holiday would fall on, here on the colonized world Oasis it was the weekend. Isabella slipped out of bed, wearing the sweatpants and oversized Del Kahn concert shirt she favored sleeping in. When she remembered Claudio had given her this shirt, which had belonged to him – reminded of this by his surprising, irritating message – she sighed with self disgust.

Remembering how she'd drank half a bottle of wine last night, after coming down from the roof, and gone to bed early, and pleasured herself and fallen into a deep sleep afterwards, she sniffed her fingers. Claudio had told her he loved the smell of her sex. She had loved his body's scents, too; armpits, balls. It was funny, she reflected, how one might be attracted in one's lover to the very kinds of smells that would repulse if it were another person.

She got to her feet, moved barefoot to her bedroom's single window, and confronted it.

The faintly glowing gold flesh was like the lid closed over a sleeping eye. When she stepped a bit closer, she could see those bubbles floating dreamily throughout it. They were mesmerizing. She tried to watch one bubble for as long as she could, as one will attempt to follow a single raindrop running down a window pane, until she finally lost track of it amongst all the others. They were like masses of people, viewed from high above, restless and wandering and lost.

Staring ahead, no longer following any particular bubble, Isabella reached out her hand in a somnambulistic way and touched a button. The lower window pane slid upwards.

Even with the pane lifted, she remained separated from the world outside. Sunlight beyond the membrane caused it to glow beyond its natural luminosity, making it translucent. It was beautiful, wasn't it? Like amber, in which some innocently passing insect might become trapped forever. In which *she* might become trapped. But what an odd thought.

Isabella reached out a hand to touch the organism, as she had done on the roof, with tentative sensitive fingertips. The hand with which she had relieved her oddly amplified hunger last night.

She felt the matter immediately push back against her. Bulge slightly into the room through the rectangular opening of the window frame. She was startled, but defied the urge to jerk her hand away. *What was this?* Again, she had a sense or intuition of a kind of longing. Or was it only her own longing, reflected back at her from this material in some way?

As if teasing a shape from very soft clay, Isabella worked her fingers – not entirely consciously – to pinch out a cone of the material. She did only half the work. It also pushed itself out, eagerly, as if *wanting* her to shape it. When this extrusion was long enough, thick enough, she slid it through her closed hand, back and forth, to smooth and further elongate it.

"Well look at you," she said dreamily, gazing down at this and smiling at it, the cylindrical shape in her lightly closed fist.

The rubbery cylinder firmed up in her hand.

Without letting go of this extrusion, lest it become absorbed back into the rest, Isabella gripped it in her right hand but jerked the waistband of her sweatpants down with her left. She had nothing on under them. She reversed her body, thrust her bared bottom out, nuzzled the protrusion against herself. Rubbed it against her until she could guide it, slide it, inside.

"Ohh God, yeah," she murmured. "Oh, fuck yeah."

She was able to let go of it now, as it was firmly slotted inside her. Though the membrane pressing through the window opening subtly pulsated, she had to provide most of the movement herself. She gripped the edges of the window frame and pushed/pulled herself. A growing rhythm. Mounting...

...quickly *exploding*.

She fell forward, onto the carpet of her bedroom, with a sobbing exclamation.

She twisted to look up from the floor, over her shoulder, at the window. At the golden membrane...as flat and inscrutable as before.

Isabella got to her feet shakily. Without a word to the flesh that blocked her view of the world beyond, she closed her window again.

She felt no sense of rebuke. Hell...rather, she almost wanted to thank it.

***

With the weekend past, it was back to work. On her way down to the ground floor of Benevento Arms on what served the planet Oasis as "Monday," Isabella boarded the lift at floor 8 to find the young man who'd once introduced himself to her as Emir, living on floor 9, leaning in a corner. *Oh God*, she thought, wishing she had retreated from the lift before the door could slide shut. With his head lowered, eyes downcast, she hadn't recognized him until it was too late. Enclosing just the two of them, the lift hissed smoothly toward the lobby.

He didn't speak to her, which rather surprised her. At a quick backward glance, Emir struck her as distracted. Isabella recalled how this tall and cocky young man with his overly virile beard and muscles had called to her and Carla on that summer evening to join him and his two friends for some drinks. And no doubt, hopefully – ultimately, inevitably – for some nice, to his mind, animalistic copulation. Isabella looked toward him again, leerily, and at last he lifted his eyes to meet hers, eyes in baggy dark sockets, only to immediately drop his gaze once more.

"Hey," she said to him, less wary of him due to this unexpected shyness. Was he less bold when sober, when not bolstered by the company of a friend?

"Hey," he replied.

"How are you? Emir, right? Floor 9?"

"I'm fine," he said hastily, almost defensively. "You're on 8?"

"Yes," she said. "Isabella"

"Nice," he stammered, as if drunk. Leaning hard into the corner as if unable to stand on his own. Not drunk, maybe, but badly hungover? "I mean...nice name."

Isabella allowed her gaze to lower. The front of the young man's pants was tented outward, and at the very tip of this display (was he even aware of it?) was a small, dark, wet stain in the fabric, as of precum.

When Isabella lifted her eyes it was to see Emir's own locked with hers. His voice sounding hesitant, uncomfortable, he asked her, "How've you been feeling? Everything okay with you?" It might have been small talk under other circumstances, but something about his tone, his edginess, made it sound like he wanted to know how she was doing *for comparison*.

"I'm fine," she told him. "Never better."

"Yeah," he said. "Yeah...me too." And he slid his body up along the wall, using it to support him, as if to prove it to her. "Just tired, you know?"

The lift reached the lobby with a ding, and when the door parted Isabella stepped out. She glanced back to see Emir hesitating at the threshold, holding out his arm to prevent the door from closing.

"You getting off?" she asked him.

"*Getting off?*" he snapped. His erection appeared more pronounced than ever, as if it were this that prevented the door from closing. "Oh...no, uh...there's something I forgot to do." He looked up toward the ceiling of the lift's cabin, dropped his arm, stepped back, and the door slid shut.

***

After work, and some errands, Isabella returned to her building and her apartment and her bedroom. It was already early evening, night's dark fluid pouring into the streets to drown them but offset their gaudy glimmerings. She found the membrane casting its mellow illumination into her room, across her bed. Like a candle glowing through honey.

Isabella didn't turn on any other lights in her room. She pushed the button to slide up the lower window pane.

She stood there, imagining how Emir had unfastened his pants or lowered his pajama bottoms and moved forward and braced his hands on the wall of his own bedroom on this same side of the building and pushed his painfully erect member into the yielding material. It would be warm, exactly like human flesh. She knew that herself.

She felt a strange and alien sorrow for what it must be like to be a man, a dumb machine cursed to be anchored to such a small but commanding organ. But right now, maybe it wasn't so alien a thought after all. She might even have better understood – if not forgiven – Claudio's stupid, selfish hunger just then.

She put out her hand, with two fingers extended and rigid like the barrel of a gun, and pressed her fingertips against the softly glowing matter with its slow-motion inner effervescence. It indented, both firm but giving at once, smooth and welcoming. The cells of which it must be made seemed to speak directly to her own components in their unified multitudes. No nation, no culture, no gender could ever be so united as the mindless cells of one living body. Such a mystery!

She worked her fingers deeply in, slid them out, in again. Did this motion excite it, as it did her? Excite all of the mass, heaped atop the roof and draped down one of the building's faces, or just this local portion of it?

Isabella sank to her knees, edged herself a little closer to the window, and leaning forward, pressed her face right into the organism. It shaped itself around her closed-eyes features. It had no scent at all, alas, not like Claudio's body. Still, with her eyes not only closed but held shut by the pressure of the matter against them, she pushed out her tongue against the rubbery but yielding material. Worked her tongue into its essence...and the two living entities mindlessly communed with each other.

Still probing her tongue into the flesh, and licking at it with increasing fervor, with one hand Isabella reached down under her waistband to stimulate herself. Her hand's circular movements became more quick and feverish, along with her tongue's desperate flickering and lunging. She inserted her fingers. Entered herself.

She came, convulsively – remembered the birds on the roof, partly sunken, fluttering their wings madly – and pressed the side of her face against the flesh so that it molded itself to her, as if to replicate her, and gasped and almost said aloud that she loved it.

How crazy is that? she thought. Was that all love was? A good, hard orgasm?

***

She didn't want to hurt the organism, but she wanted even more than it had given her...though by now – days since her first communion with it – she had taken it into her mouth, into her two lower orifices. She wanted a portion of it to *live* in her, if only briefly, like the sperm of a man.

Isabella fetched a utility knife with a beam rather than a blade, that her father had added into a little tool box he'd cutely put together for her like some housewarming gift, and brought it to the bedroom. She undressed slowly, ritualistically, as if this were some ceremony, as if this thing *watched* her. Then she stepped to the open window. She coaxed out an extrusion, a protrusion, of the luminous matter…teased it into something she could hold in her left hand. And then, with her right hand, she positioned the silently sizzling red beam over the root of it.

Before she could touch beam to flesh, she looked up and saw a dark silhouette, in the shape of a man, sliding down through the organism's body. Headfirst…but unlike a diver into water, his arms were spread out as if to gather sensation. Isabella couldn't make out his features, but she took this slowly descending figure to be Emir. He, too, must have cut into the body of the organism with a beam or blade. But, rather than with the intension of inserting a piece of the matter into himself, he had chosen to insert himself into the matter.

Isabella watched his silhouette float down slowly, inside the glowing flesh – until he descended out of her range of sight – before she applied the red beam and cut into it, herself.

***

The next evening, upon returning to Benevento Arms after work and a few errands, plastic grocery bags like extra organs of her body slung from one hand, Isabella stepped out of her cab onto the sidewalk, tilted her head back to look up, and exclaimed, " No! Oh God!"

She could only assume these workers were health agents, or at least low level employees of the Health Agency of Paxton. Come at long last.

A kind of platform hovered in the air near the roof of the building.

Perched on a narrow walkway that ran around the top of this floating platform, workers garbed in baggy black rubbery suits and hoods with face plates were using long poles like bo staffs to cut into the organism that was draped over the side of Benevento Arms. The poles' red-glowing tips indicated they were a type of beam cutter instrument, themselves.

Isabella would know nothing of ancient Earth sailors using flensing tools to cut into the bodies of an extinct marine animal called a whale, harpooned and brought up alongside their whaling vessel, but a historian might have made that comparison.

A claw arm, having extended from the platform, gripped a slab of the organism's matter – as Isabella had gripped a far smaller extrusion of it the day before – and held it until, with repeated applications of their poles, the HAP workers had severed it completely. Then, careful not to strike the workers and knock them over the railing of their walkway, the mechanical arm shifted to carry the severed slab toward the center of the platform, where it was lowered down. But the platform didn't appear to be deep enough to store this great chunk of meat. No, Isabella knew, it was a huge zapper unit, a much bigger version of the zapper she used in her own kitchen to dispose of garbage and non-recyclable trash. She could even hear from down here, despite the noise of the city, the platform sizzle like frying grease as it disintegrated the slab.

They were hovering near the top of the building, and had already cleared almost all of the matter that had hung down one face of the building. Soon all that would be left to deal with was the material on the roof, including those curious exposed rings with their spiraling centers.

Isabella turned to lunge toward the front doors of Benevento Arms, and then paused when she noticed a cluster of several hover vehicles parked to one side of the building. They were black, with the HAP logo in gold on their flanks, and one of them had the appearance of an ambulance. But an ambulance that was in no hurry to be along its way to a hospital. It was then that Isabella realized what had finally brought the Health Agency people here.

Why hadn't she considered, yesterday, that Emir might not survive giving himself wholly to the organism? Why hadn't she called the police then and there? She wondered if it had begun to digest him, or if he had only suffocated inside it.

Either way, she had no doubt that whatever was left of him lay in the back of that HAP ambulance right now.

***

Though she had seen it from the street, she still needed to see it from within her apartment, within her bedroom...

Her window was now cleared, returned to its unobstructed view of the city called Punktown. There was no point in opening the pane; she would only hear, but louder, the sizzling bursts of the floating zapper as more flesh was fed into it. She depressed a button beside the window to shade its panes to black.

Even as night fell in earnest, the workers continued on up there, by the lights of their platform and the city's multicolored ambient light. They had apparently brought the hover platform to rest on the rooftop.

Though she was reluctant at first to remove it from the shelter of her body, her curiosity got the better of her, and Isabella disrobed from the waist down, cupped a hand between her legs, and willed her little pet out of her. It obeyed, oozed into her palm, and she lifted it to examine it. It still maintained its subtle ambery glow, throbbed with life. She put her pet into a deep bowl she had placed on her bedside table, where it continued to pulse but made no attempt to climb the bowl's smooth wall to escape.

But when she checked in on it an hour later, after having eaten her dinner, at the bottom of the bowl she found a grayish, withered and dry-looking object that gave off the stench of decomposition, like a dead mouse found under a bed.

By that time – Isabella would later learn – the brassy rings had been fully extracted from the material that remained on the roof, severing their connection to it. The platform had lowered the rings to the street and, via its claw arm, loaded them into the back of a HAP hover van to be borne away...either to return them to the people who owned the organic ship from which the mass had sloughed off, or to be destroyed.

Her eyes wet, her body empty, Isabella dumped the gray mass from the bowl into a little white box with a cover that had contained a pair of new earrings. On the cover, in a red pen, she drew a heart like a valentine. Then, she placed the box into her kitchen's trash zapper, and pressed its button.

OUT OF NOTHING

Part 1

The neighborhood its residents called Segundo Inferno was one of the worst slums in the city of Punktown, vying with Warehouse Way, the Battery, and the mutant ghetto Tin Town. The original low-income apartment blocks here had been added onto over the decades, bristling with tumor-like mini-blocks on their roofs and flanks, with new boxes formed of various materials ever being added onto these. Seldom were building permits pursued, or violations brought against these improvised structures. Though struts and cables helped support them, occasionally one of them tore loose and crashed to the street. Once, such a cube had toppled from its precarious perch atop a stack of gaily pastel-painted and mural-slathered boxes and become wedged between two lower boxes, suspended above the street at a height that still allowed ground traffic to pass beneath it. Its tenants had continued living on in it in this new orientation.

Gangs ran this enclave, selling drugs and managing prostitution, fighting over micro-territories like dogs over shreds of meat. Thieves stealing to survive in this harsh environment, if caught not only by the gangs but by common citizens, would have their hands shot clean through, at the very least, or might be beaten to death or burned alive in the street. Enemy gang members – whether male or female or adolescent – would be captured and tortured, dismembered alive with machetes or axes or laser blades, before finally being beheaded, vids of these acts being shared as a warning on the net (or even on the ultranet, to be more immersively experienced by those who could afford that virtual reality service).

A man named Antonio dos Santos da Silva, who had been born in Segundo Inferno but had worked hard to leave it behind and had become a successful small business owner beyond the slum's reach, had returned to try to encourage other residents to follow his lead. He held gatherings in schools and churches, even on street corners. He distributed flyers door to door. He left holographic placards hovering in the air, with his inspiring words ever scrolling. Instead of killing each other, he passionately entreated, the citizens of Segundo Inferno should be working together, lifting each other up! No one was going to do it for them; nobody outside this enclave was sufficiently concerned. (The forcers had almost no presence here, and even the big crime syndys didn't care enough to try to control the drug traffic in this small if overpopulated carcinoma.) The citizens, da Silva said, should be helping repair and fortify their neighbors' ramshackle homes. They should band together to open little food markets, other shops and businesses. With cooperation and a sense of pride, they could overcome their circumstances and make this neighborhood thrive!

But one night the nice Punktown apartment of Antonio dos Santos da Silva was broken into by three young men who had ventured forth from Segundo Inferno, and he and his wife and two children were messily stabbed and bludgeoned to death, because he had innocently happened to mention at a recent gathering that for Christmas he had given his eldest daughter Part 3 of the toy called Ex nihilo.

Part 2

Rich or poor, human colonist or native Choom, it seemed that everyone on the planet Oasis now wanted Ex nihilo.

Was it a toy, really? A decoration, an entertainment, a distraction? The VT commercial went like this:

Every day we're bombarded with news...assaulted with information. Burdened with overwhelming concerns that don't allow us a sense of peace, responsibilities that deny us a degree of harmony.

Are you tired of this excess of meaning?

Ex nihilo. Because it makes no demands. It has no meaning.

Part 3

Matheus da Silva dos Santos lay back on his bed in his darkened bedroom, while outside his window – the pane of which he had tinted black to block the glare of winter sun – he heard the commotion dying down in the street below. A few minutes ago he had looked out to determine its source, and had seen a ring of young men striking at a fallen figure with machetes and bats and pipes. From up here, the figure, probably already dead, had looked like a gray-skinned Kalian, but it was hard to tell for all the blood. Was the fool new to Punktown? Had he never heard about Segundo Inferno's keenly enforced homogeneous character? Its inhabitants prided themselves on it, in a city that was famous for being a melting pot of human and nonhuman races. Only in this sort of enterprise, the act of killing outsiders or maiming petty thieves, did the community seem to come together in something like what the late Antonio dos Santos da Silva had preached.

Matheus da Silva dos Santos was one of the three young men who had killed da Silva and his family for Part 3 of Ex nihilo.

Da Silva had not possessed Parts 1 and 2, and neither did Matheus; he had only seen what they looked like, and the light effects they projected, on the net. But at this moment he lay staring up at the ceiling of his bedroom with Part 3 resting on the floor beside his shoes, looking like an abstracted black insect, perhaps, made of some material he couldn't identify. Plastic? Metal? Some substance beyond his comprehension? If he had possessed either – or better yet, both – Parts 1 or 2, they would fit together with Part 3 with satisfying clicks, forming a whole new shape, and the light the connected parts projected would have been combined to form even more complex designs.

From a pinhole in the uppermost point of Part 3 it projected a beam, casting upon the ceiling a dreamily moving, roughly circular patch of pure white light, like an ever-changing spiderweb of glowing ectoplasm, a web that slowly but ceaselessly folded/unfolded into new webs, an interweaving lace of colorless fractals. It was like looking through the tube of a kaleidoscope. It was profoundly relaxing. It was perplexing, too, in an intriguing and nonthreatening way, like visions he had experienced using various hallucinogenic drugs.

At first, another of the three gang members who had stolen Part 3 from da Silva had held onto the thing (because Matheus was wary about being investigated as da Silva's killer), until they could find someone who would pay them good money for the increasingly rare collectible, but then Matheus had learned from a snitch that his friend – Hugo Sousa dos Santos – had made an attempt to sell Part 3 on his own. The snitch, who sought Matheus' favor, said that Hugo had intended to tell Matheus the piece had been stolen from him.

Yesterday, Matheus and several others in their gang had lured Hugo into the basement of Matheus' home, and there set upon him. They had begun making a vid of his torture and execution, to share on the net so as to let the world (and the others in their gang) know that Matheus, their leader, did not take betrayal lightly. While Matheus was sawing into Hugo's throat with a kitchen knife, and speaking ominously to the camera, his mother had called down the basement stairs, "Sweet Jesus, what is all that noise?"

"Fuck, Mamãe!" Matheus had bellowed. "You're ruining my vid!"

"Don't you swear at me, you little monster!" his mother had shouted, coming halfway down the stairs. "Oh dear God, not again! Do you expect me to clean this mess?" And she had looked accusingly at the desperate eyes of Hugo. Then she'd cried in horror, "Is that my bread knife?"

Matheus knew that despite this demonstration, others in his gang might yet betray him. More likely still was that another gang might attack him, even force its way into his home and kidnap his mother, his sister, in order to win possession of Part 3 of Ex nihilo, so it was really in his best interest to sell it to someone as quickly as he could.

The more he gazed at that mesmerizing play of light upon the theater screen of his ceiling, however, the more regret he felt at the idea of parting with the enigmatic little black gizmo.

Despite the advertisements saying upfront that Ex nihilo had no meaning, he wasn't sure he bought into that. He felt there was something hidden in that hypnotic display of light. A code of some kind, that weirdly seemed to speak to him personally…that sought to impart an intimate message directly to his soul. If that hollow space he sometimes became all too conscious of, inside him, could be called a soul.

Part 4

"Are you out of your blasting *mind*, you morbidly obese, dung-stinking, lobotomized drooler?"

Djane thrust toward her father the small white thing that was almost a figurine, or part of a figurine, she had only a moment before excitedly unwrapped from its velvet-lined box. "This isn't Ex nihilo!"

"No, honey," stammered her father, Vic Klimenko, owner of Nepenthouse, a very popular nightclub on the top floor of an office building in Punktown's upscale Beaumonde Square. He had dressed in his very best five-piece business suit of Ramon silk for the occasion of his daughter's sweet sixteen birthday party. Over a hundred guests had been invited. Now, despite his attire he looked rather less than dignified with his jaw hanging slack, Djane's young guests less than celebratory as they too gaped like witnesses to a calamitous hoverbus accident. Klimenko's hulking, usually impassive bodyguard Popov shifted his stance uncomfortably, and even the twin robots that had been tending to the buffet table seemed to stare in paralyzed dread at the father and his tiny, thin, terribly beautiful daughter with her dark hair slicked back close to her exquisite head and her long graceful neck stretched taut and her blue eyes bulging madly and her full, gore-red lips forming a twisted frame around badly overlapping teeth. Her teeth had once been perfectly straight, but the Japanese called this cutely crooked look *yaeba* and it was currently in vogue. Klimenko had reluctantly paid his dentist to have this work done a few months ago.

"Honey," he went on, "I went to four places, and I looked on the net, and I couldn't find Part 3 of Ex nihilo anywhere. It's sold out here on Oasis, baby – that's what everyone tells me. You know they only make it in limited numbers."

"I'm not as dumb as you are, you pathetic nut-sack!" Djane screeched at him. "I *know* it's a limited series! But it isn't so limited that my supposedly wealthy and connected father shouldn't be able to find Part 3 somewhere, somehow, when common blue collar kids and even *fucking mutants* have somehow managed to get their hands on it!"

"I know, sweetie, but they got there first...I didn't know that's what you wanted until it was too late!"

"So what the blast is *this?*" She threw the white sort-of-figurine at her father's chest. It bounced off his shimmering vest, clattered to the dance floor of Nepenthouse, where her party was being held. In striking the floor, the delicate white device projected a beam of moving, multiple colors, restless blobs of superimposed and ever-blending colors that swarmed like single cell organisms viewed under a microscope. Those guests upon whose legs the light fell edged backwards as if these undesired colors might taint them. Ex nihilo's light was *white*.

"It's called Nuttin, babe," Klimenko said, with a kind of desperation. "It's even better than Ex nihilo, they told me! Ex nihilo is only going to have five parts by the time it's finished! Nuttin has ten...*ten*, sweetie! A new part released every month, and I swear I'll get you each and every one of them!"

"It...is...not...the same...fucking...*thing!* It's a cheap knockoff...it's like an imitation Yazata handbag! How can you humiliate me in front of my friends like this, you fucking child-molesting warthog?"

Klimenko's face flushed red. He feared Djane's friends might think she was accusing him of molesting her, when he knew she was digging him about his second wife, twenty-five years his junior. He envied his wife for having found an excuse not to attend the party today...and Djane's mother was safely distant on Earth, unable to get away for her own dubious reasons. He felt like a sacrificed soldier, sent first onto the minefield while his comrades watched from their trenches.

"I'm sorry, hon."

"*Sorry?*" Djane screamed. "You tell me, what good are Parts 1 and 2 if I don't get 3? There's no point in me getting 4 and 5, is there? It's all ruined – it will never be complete! What do you want me to do with 1 and 2 now, fuck myself in the ass with them?"

"I..." Klimenko couldn't say more, feeling close to tears.

Djane stomped over to Part 1 of Nuttin, where it lay on its side on the floor like an albino mantis, projecting its colors sideways instead of onto the ceiling as it – and Ex nihilo – was intended to do, and crushed it under her foot. Its pointy edges poked her flesh through the thin sole of her expensive ballet-like slipper.

"Ow!" she wailed, bursting into hopeless sobs, her delicate shoulders shaking. "*Fuuuck!*"

Part 5

Was this a conspiracy, Djane Klimenko wondered, concocted by cynical and sadistic corporate types, taking delight in torturing naive and trusting consumers?

She sliced a third line across the upper part of her right thigh, using a laser pen. The three shallow slices resembled the claw mark of an animal. She watched dew drops of blood poke their way to the surface, spaced along these three lines like beads on an abacus.

Transfixed by the blood, and the hot sparkly pain, she was able to ground herself...to stop hyperventilating. But though she had got her breathing and her sobbing under control, the great bitterness still percolated inside her, a burning bile of the mind.

Why, when one bought Part 1 of Ex nihilo, was some kind of subscription not offered – a means of ordering the next four parts in advance? It was not a speculation...she *knew*, from reading forlorn complaints on the net, complaints that were not just expressions of frustration but of utter despair, that there were people who had only been able to acquire Part 1...Parts 1 and 2...only Part 2...only Parts 2 and 3, the latest. Or 1 and 3. Someone would have Part 1 and some stranger would have what should be their Part 2, like orphaned siblings separated forever.

Yes, it was true: each portion of Ex nihilo was supposedly designed to be its own distinct entity. One could, the company insisted, have only one piece and be content with that. One could match 3 with 1, 5 with 2, and so on, and leave it at that. Each individual unit, and each combination of those units, delivered its own experience. But who were they trying to kid? They had labeled the pieces 1 through 5, hadn't they? The implication being that the series had to be followed sequentially and *completed*. No, Djane swore, they *wanted* to make the process of gathering every piece difficult. It increased the desire, the desperation, to own them. It kept people talking...it generated publicity...it made people want what the company itself touted was *meaningless*.

"You watch," her mother had tried to comfort her, in a vid call from Earth earlier tonight after the guests had all left Nepenthouse. "About six months after Part 5 comes out, they'll offer a second batch of Parts 1 through 5, all together in one package."

"But that would be a *second* edition of Ex nihilo," Djane had lamented. "Not the first blasting edition!"

Djane wondered if there was a secret meaning to Ex nihilo, after all – or at least, an ultimate purpose. That being, to inspire widespread madness. A maddened consumer is a vulnerable, a malleable consumer.

She felt a fresh sob rising up in her throat, like a bubble of toxic gas that threatened to ascend to her brain and pop. "I won't be your puppet," she groaned, flicking on the red glowing tip of the laser utility pen again. She pulled up on the left cuff of the short-shorts she slept in.

But instead of lowering the laser blade to her unmarked left thigh, she turned her gaze to her bedroom's idle computer station. On the corner of the desk upon which it sat rested Parts 1 and 2 of Ex nihilo, snapped together to form a new design like mating lovers. Their combined beam currently sent churning, overlapping, patternless patterns of white light across her ceiling, creating one unique and fleeting snowflake-like design after another. Sometimes, though she realized it was illogical, she swore she saw her name spelled out in the chaos before it dissolved again. What more might she glimpse if she had Parts 3...4...5?

"Comp on," Djane demanded haughtily. In the air above her computer system, a holographic screen spread open. "Prepare to search."

"What is it we're looking for tonight, sexy?" the comp's voice (that of a teenage vid actor Djane currently had a crush on) asked her.

"Search for anyone looking to sell Part 3 of Ex nihilo – any price. If my father knows what's good for him, he'll pay it. I don't believe him that he's already tried this...there has to be *someone* willing to part with Part 3. Someone more desperate for cash than they are for Ex nihilo."

"I'll search every shopping site I can find, cutie," the disembodied voice assured her.

"Not just shopping sites, you twat – forums, social media sites, everything. Leave no turn unstoned, or whatever they say."

"You got it, sweet cheeks," the machine promised.

Part 6

The Coleopteroids, more commonly referred to as Bedbugs, were an extradimensional race that were more or less giant beetles walking on their hindmost pair of legs, but for interactions with human/oid races they used "liaisons" that were either bioengineered entities in the form of humans or, as many suspected, repurposed human corpses. From one such liaison Matheus regularly obtained the drug called purple vortex that his gang would portion out and sell in Segundo Inferno. Because the Bedbug liaisons knew better than to set foot – or claw – in the aggressively retained territory of Segundo Inferno itself, these transactions always took place in a restroom of a coffee shop across the street from that neighborhood; one of the JavaJunky chain found throughout the city.

By law there could be no security cams installed in a restroom, so Matheus made his usual exchange therein and was relived when the eerie, unsettling liaison – seeming to glide a little off the floor in its long black robe – pushed its way out through the door. For his part, the bag of glittering purple vortex stuffed into a pocket in his jacket lining, Matheus turned to relieve himself further at a urinal. When his wrist comp beeped to announce an incoming call, he cursed under his breath and stuffed himself away more quickly than he'd intended.

He looked down into the little screen of the device strapped to his left wrist. He'd stolen this, too, from the home of Antonio dos Santos da Silva. The screen read *Unknown Caller*, the individual's image blocked. Rather than open the call, he chose to let the person begin leaving a message.

"Hi...my name is Jane Pachinko," the caller said. The voice was distorted by a filter, Matheus could tell, but it would seem to be a young she. Didn't mean it really was, though. The person went on, "I saw your ad on Netshops. You say you have a Part 3 of Ex nihilo for sale? If this is true, please call me as soon as possible at this number, and –"

Matheus decided to take the call, though he had his image blocked on his end, as well. "Yeah, Jane? This is, uh, Matt. You're right, I got a Part 3 for sale. But I ain't blasting around, here."

"Me neither, buddo," said the young voice. "What are you asking?"

"Ten thousand munits."

The voice barked a short, hard laugh. "Blast you, drooler, that's insane. What are you really asking for it?"

If a man called him a drooler to his face Matheus would gouge out his eyes with the tip of a machete, but somehow this (apparent) young female caller's toughness was almost like a flirtation to his ears. "This thing is rare, baby. I'm not surprised there's not enough money in your piggybank to cover it."

"I'll get you five thousand munits. That's the most I'll offer...the most anyone has asked for Part 3, that I've seen, and even that's crazy."

"Five thousand?" He hadn't really expected ten...hadn't expected five, even. He had begun to feel the faintest twinge of regret (if not quite guilt) for having killed that entire family for the thing. This, and his unexpected attachment to the mysterious little doodad, had made him wonder if he should just hang onto it, after all (maybe telling people he had already sold it just to keep them from killing him for it).

"I guarantee I'll have it," the caller said, with the authority of a much older person. And maybe she was?

Despite Matheus' wariness – for his dealings always entailed wariness – they made arrangements. Tomorrow they would meet here, at this very JavaJunky, his usual transaction point...and then he would see if the piggybank of this "Jane" was as fat as she claimed.

Part 7

"Sweetie, it's not smart at all...let *me* go pay this person for Part 3," Vic Klimenko implored, reaching out toward his daughter but not daring to quite touch her as she slipped into her winter coat. "Me and Popov."

"*Not smart?*" Djane echoed. "As in, you think I'm stupid, like you? Of course Popov is going – with me. You didn't half try to get me Part 3 for my birthday, and you embarrassed me in front of all my friends, so now it's time to let me handle things."

"And I told you I'm sorry for that, and I'll pay the five thousand, but this isn't safe, hon!"

"I can take care of myself. Me, and Popov." She whirled at the looming bodyguard. "So are you coming or not, dumbass?"

Klimenko sighed, and nodded at Popov. "Please watch out for her, will you?"

The giant of a bodyguard nodded. He was bald, a spiral with an eye at its center tattooed on his forehead, its lines radiating out across his face until they seemed to slip past the confines of his flesh. "Of course, sir," he grunted.

"Then let's do this," Djane snapped, glaring at her father defiantly, holding out her hand for the money.

Not trusting her with his card, nor trusting this Matt person to exchange money from that card to his own, Klimenko counted off fifty one-hundred-munit bills into her hand. "Happy birthday again, honey," he said, wanting to wince as he handed her the last bill.

She stuffed the wad into her pocketbook, and bared her expensively defective teeth at him sweetly. "I love you,

Daddy," she said in a sing-song voice, such as that of a possessed doll in a horror movie.

Part 8

When the floating holographic light changed to indicate it was safe to use the crosswalk, Matheus walked toward the JavaJunky in front of which this Jane had agreed to meet him. He was seemingly alone, but a half hour ago he had sent two of his people ahead of him. Gabriel Herrera dos Santos – the snitch who had alerted him about the traitorous Hugo, eager to further prove his value to the gang leader – sat at a table inside JavaJunky, near the window, with a handgun in his pocket. A more seasoned gang member, Bruno Pereira da Silva, stood out on the sidewalk not far from the door to JavaJunky, pretending to chat with someone on his wrist comp (this one, too, stolen from the home of Antonio dos Santos da Silva). In reality, his wrist comp and Matheus' were currently linked so Bruno could monitor the deal.

Idling at the curb directly in front of the coffee shop, hovering above the pavement, was a black limo with black-tinted windows. Matheus had been told to look for this vehicle, and he walked toward it warily. It looked like something out of a syndy movie.

Inside the hoverlimo, in the back seat, Djane watched Matheus cross the street and said to Popov through the screen that separated the front seat from the passenger area, "That's him – that's Matt. He told me he'd be wearing a shiny green jacket and yellow running pants."

"Great," said Popov. "He's coming from Segundo Inferno...did you see that?"

"Coming from Whatty-What?"

"It's one of the worst of the worst slums in Punktown, Miss Klimenko."

"Oh yeah? It does look like quite the mountain of shit, over there. Never heard of it...I've never been to this part of Punktown before."

"And for good reason. We shouldn't be here now."

"Just keep your opinions to yourself and keep an eye on this kid." The young man in the metallic green jacket had almost reached them. "I'm going to let him in."

Matheus leaned down and rapped lightly on a passenger window, grinning to disguise his ill-ease. He wore a backpack with Part 3 of Ex nihilo in it, and a pistol was hidden in his rear waistband. "Hello?" he called through the opaque window.

Djane appraised his appearance. He was in his early twenties, with short curly black hair and a wall of bright teeth. He had a holographic tattoo of a teardrop that rolled from the corner of his right eye down his cheek in a continuous animated loop, and a holographic tattoo across the front of his throat that was seemingly a deep gash pouring an animated flow of blood. She found these embellishments tacky but weirdly attractive at the same time, enhancing his more natural attributes: high cheekbones, full sexy lips, and droopy-lidded soulless eyes.

She touched a keypad on the armrest beside her and the window went from black to clear. Smiling out at him, she said, "Well hi, Matt. I'm Jane."

Matheus was surprised. The girl *was* a girl, and just as young as she'd sounded despite the voice filter. He felt relief, and his smile became more genuine, especially since the girl was beautiful, classy-looking with her dark slicked hair and vivid red lips...though she could really use a dentist to straighten those crooked teeth.

"Hey, Jane! I believe I have something for you."

She responded sweetly, "And I hope that 'something' is Part 3 of Ex nihilo, and not some nasty surprise that would get you killed by my driver."

Matheus chuckled nervously, and glanced at the driver's still black-tinted window. Was she the daughter of a syndy gangster? She herself had the bearing of a crime boss in the making. He hadn't entertained the notion of robbing this person for the money and simply keeping Part 3, and he entertained that notion even less now. "Hey, baby, I'm on the level here."

She touched another key to unlock the rear door, and slid aside to give him room to enter. "Then get on in here, buddo."

Matheus complied, and shut the door after him. Looking up front, through the security screen he saw the spiral-tattooed face of the girl's driver/bodyguard turned around to glower at him. "Hey, man," Matheus said. "No worries...I'm cool. Great tattoo." Though Matheus thought it would be that much greater if the spiral was animated, always spinning hypnotically.

"So..." Djane prompted him.

"Right." He slipped off his backpack and unfastened its flap, from the corner of his eye watching that driver, afraid that if he moved too abruptly he'd get himself shot. The driver hadn't lowered the security screen, so Matheus was thinking he probably had a blaster that could fire a killing beam right through the glass without disturbing it.

He lifted out an unmarked black box, then opened its hinged lid to reveal Part 3 of *Ex nihilo*, nestled in its velvet-lined hollow within. Djane wagged her head, as if in awe. "So you weren't scamming me. How did a sleazy little slum rat like you come by this? Or should I ask?"

"Don't ask, beautiful."

"*Beautiful*, huh?" She narrowed her eyes as if she disbelieved his compliment, but her smile had grown larger. "Now, it works and all, right?"

"Whatever it is this thing is supposed to do, it does it. See?" And with that, he reached into the box and activated the tiny projecting lens in the uppermost portion of the gadget. Immediately, the ceiling of the hoverlimo's interior became awash in celestial light, one roughly circular shape blooming after the next, flowers that opened and dissolved, with thin spokes turning slowly clockwise, then fat arms turning slowly counterclockwise, snowflake-shape melting into spiderweb-lattice, then another spinning white whorl. A silent vortex of light that almost instantly mesmerized the both of them, so that for several seconds they just tilted back their heads watching it without speaking, bonded in the empty experience.

Finally, Djane said, "Good work, my friend...good work."

"Do you have Parts 1 and 2?"

"Oh yes. You?"

"No. I sure would love to see the three parts connected. Never seen it in person. Think you could show me sometime?"

"Oh, so you're asking me for a date now, is that it, Matt?" She reached to take the box off his lap but he closed the lid, cutting off the light, and folded his hands atop it.

"What if I am?" He grinned again.

"Hm. I might consider that...if you lower the price for that there."

"Lower it to what?"

"To free. You give that to me for free, and I'll give you a date."

Matheus laughed. "Baby, you're gorgeous and all, but a five thousand munit date?"

"How about if we have our date right here, right now?" Before he could answer, she said to her driver, "Turn your screen opaque, Popov."

"I can't do that, Miss Klimenko."

"You do that or I'll have your job, you pea-brained son of a mutant whore. Do it *now*."

"As you wish, Miss Klimenko. But your friend should be advised that I'm a veteran of the Red War. I have forty-two confirmed kills...thirty-five of them in the Red War."

"I told you, brother, I'm cool."

The barrier dividing driver's area from passenger's area went black.

Djane turned back to Matheus. "So...ready for a date?" Her fingers, tipped blood red, began unfastening the collar of her blouse.

"Damn," Matheus said, as hypnotized by those fingers as he had been by the light display. "Listen...there's a lot of hot meat in that place I live, but I never had a girl like you. If it was just me, I'd say blast it, forget the money. But I have two friends waiting for me to make this deal, and I promised them a thousand munits each. I can't stiff them."

"Hm," Djane said, noticing that he had set the box down on the far side of him and was unfastening the front of his yellow running pants. "Talk about stiff. Okay, Matt...you strike a hard bargain – *very* hard, I see – but I'll pay you three thousand. A thousand for the three of you, and two thousand for me that my Daddy doesn't need to know I hung onto. And he doesn't need to know about *this*, either." And with that, she bent down over him.

Part 9

When they had stared together like lovers in bed at the light show on the limo's ceiling, Matheus could have sworn he saw stroboscopic words flicker to him briefly, that spelled out the message: *Love her.*

Djane had thought she's seen black words, too, in the empty gaps between crystalline spikes of white light, that spelled out the words: *Kill him*.

While her lowered head pistoned, her right hand drew from her pocketbook the laser pen she used to slice into her own flesh when she was stressed. She drew back her head, still gripping him in her left hand, and swept in with the right – the utility knife's beam thumbed to its maximum intensity.

Matheus screamed, his cry amplified deafeningly in the limo's enclosed space. "X marks the spot," Djane said, sitting up and slashing at the animated tattoo on his throat. Real blood and holographic blood blended, indistinguishable. "Popov!" she shouted. "Get us out of here!"

Already she was thinking of what she might do with five thousand munits. Put them aside for Parts 4 and 5? This time she wouldn't wait for her clueless father to acquire them for her; she'd buy them herself as soon as they were released, when they only went for about five hundred munits apiece.

Matheus had fallen back hard against the door, one hand clutching at his neck as if to staunch its flow, the other reaching around behind him. Was he trying to find the keypad to get the door open? Still holding the laser knife in her right hand, Djane snapped out her left and grabbed hold of the box containing Part 3.

To think she would actually let this slum rat, however cute, fuck her like one of those pieces of "hot meat" in his inbred ghetto! Sheer comedy!

"What's going on back there?" Popov shouted.

"I said go! We've got to dump this punk somewhere!"

From behind his back, Matheus pulled a compact .55 semiautomatic, loaded with solid projectiles rather than gel capsules filled with corrosive plasma. Matheus appreciated the carnal allure of blood; he liked to punch holes, to tear meat. This was what he did, when he fired four shots into Djane's face and her cutely crooked teeth, point blank. Right before he did so she protested, "Hey!" as if this was a cheat, as if someone of his rank could not possibly kill her, but he did. Djane's blood and brain matter and clumps of gelled hair splatted against the inside of the hoverlimo.

Hearing the shots over his wrist comp's open channel, Bruno Pereira da Silva dashed toward the idling vehicle. As he ran, he drew his own handgun. Seeing this from inside JavaJunky, the new boy, Gabriel the snitch, bolted up from his table and lunged toward the door.

Bruno's gun, a blaster, fired short red beams, like crossbow quarrels, right through the limo's black-tinted windshield blindly. Over the wrist comp, he had heard the driver say he was an experienced killer, and he knew to take him out first.

One might question why Popov decided to exit the hovering limo, if *decided* is the right word, when part of the man's skull was seared away, his eye under that smoking trough hanging dislodged on his cheek. Had he been safer inside, or trapped? Was he too vulnerable out on the street, or did he have a chance to flee? Running at him, Bruno kept firing ray bolts at and through him, though some missed and glanced off passing traffic. Spun around by one such bolt, Popov faced Gabriel just as he burst out onto the sidewalk from JavaJunky, pistol in hand. Gabriel was young and inexperienced, and took too long to take aim, and just before Popov collapsed to the street dead he extended his own blaster and speared one red beam into the boy's forehead. They dropped together.

Bruno, the only survivor of the incident, shoved his gun back into his coat pocket and charged toward the street to return to Segundo Inferno. He was too hasty, however, and halfway through the crosswalk the pedestrian light changed and he didn't survive, after all, as a speeding hovercar struck him and threw him back toward the sidewalk like some mere toy.

Part 10

Less than a year after the incident that occurred on the street between Segundo Inferno and JavaJunky, some months after Part 5 of Ex nihilo had been released, it came to be that the hot new collectible was the ten-part toy called Nuttin.

Part 1 was particularly rare and coveted.

LITTLE WING

1: Mr. Dolor

"Show me the fairy."

Osman Ginko stepped back to let the new arrival enter the "safe" apartment he had arranged to use for this transaction. He turned from the door and started down a hallway toward the last of the unoccupied flat's three bedrooms. He wouldn't have turned his back on this guest, who went by the name Mr. Dolor, had Ginko's partner O'lz not been present to follow after Mr. Dolor in turn. O'lz was a female KeeZee, an odd albino specimen, seven feet tall as was the norm but the film of flesh sucked tight to her fearsome-jawed head was clear instead of gray-black, her veins showing vividly through it. Her dreadlocks were white instead of black, her three tiny eyes pink instead of black. She never spoke; she was wont to let her assault engine, currently gripped in both fists, handle any important communication.

The walls of the hallway, and its floor and ceiling – as in every room of the apartment, in fact – were double sheets of clear plastic. Sandwiched between them was an orange gel with a subtle, constant glow. A species of black worm, the largest specimens over a foot long, had once tunneled through this nourishing gel, not serving any practical purpose but just part of the decor. However, the thousands of worms had long since all sickened and died, their shriveled carcasses entombed in the mazes of burrows they had made. Before Mr. Dolor's arrival, gesturing at one wall, Ginko had joked to O'lz, "This will be Punktown one day…when we've all killed each other off." Punktown was the nickname of this city, and Punktowners were ravenously hungry, as these worms had been.

A long nail was driven into the closed door to the third bedroom, and from it hung two military-style gas masks with goggles. Ginko took them down and passed one to Mr. Dolor, saying, "Here – put this on."

Mr. Dolor hesitated, then handed his mask back. "I need to know what this is like, firsthand."

"It's like a lot," warned Ginko.

"Okay," said Mr. Dolor. "I should hope so." He jerked his chin at the KeeZee. "What about her?"

"Not all races are affected."

"I see." Now Dolor nodded at the door. "Open it."

"As you like." Ginko hung Dolor's mask by its strap again, fitted his own mask onto his head, then opened the door and led his guest inside.

A kitchen table stood in the room's center, the only piece of furniture in the apartment at this time. Upon it rested a large metal cylinder, which Ginko went to stand beside. Dolor stopped at its foot. "Ready?" asked Ginko.

"Go," said Dolor, glancing from one to the other of the two windows in the room. Their panes had been adjusted to a full black tint for privacy. He realized this was bound to be embarrassing.

Ginko touched a key on the cylinder's side, and its topmost portion slid away, curved down into the lower portion. Dolor leaned forward for a better look at its contents, even as Ginko pressed another key that set two fans in the floor of the cylinder to spinning, wafting a soft breeze up into Dolor's face...bringing with it an odd musty smell, brown and aged in character, like crispy autumn leaves, a squashed forest mushroom, a pile of old newspapers, but with something else in the mix: a muskiness that was not decay, that had resisted decay. A scent that was vital and immediate...inexplicably universal and eternal.

Resting in the little coffin was an odd, anthropomorphic figure, small as a child. Mummified, desiccated, its skeletal frame seemingly spray-painted with a thin coating of skin. Its flesh was gray, its half-open eyes intact and entirely black, its dark lips withered away from a crazed grin of yellow teeth. Its forehead sloped back radically, the rear of the elongated skull tapering almost to a point. Crossed upon its chest were two wings, now dry parchments but once supple membranes growing down from the lower arms to the outsides of the legs.

Osman Ginko – purveyor of dubious and ill-gotten rarities, skilled at relating their histories and virtues – explained, "The Fahleet have been extinct for over a hundred years. They were a primitive tribe on Kali – a peaceful people overall, from all accounts – but the Kalians saw them as offensive savages, if not outright demons because of their wings, so they systematically wiped them out over the years. You know the Kalians. Funny, though, how they used parts of their bodies as icons. Wind chimes and flutes made out of their hollow bones. Plenty of old books, even copies of their holy book the *Fizala*, used Fahleet wing leather for their covers. Not that they really flew...they glided."

"Ohh," said Dolor, but it didn't sound like an acknowledgement of Ginko's informative discourse. It sounded like the start of a moan. He hadn't taken his eyes off the mummy. The folded wings left a gap between them that revealed the long-dead entity to have been a female.

"And then," Ginko went on, watching the man through his goggles, "there were the bodies that were preserved in whole, like this one."

"I can picture them," Dolor said dreamily, as if speaking under hypnosis. "I can see them clearly...like a vid in my head. They built houses up in the trees...higher and higher up, in taller and taller trees, as the Kalians worked to exterminate them."

"Yes," Ginko confirmed.

"They protected their young in their shelters, taught them their language. *I can hear it!*" Dolor shivered. "They glided from tree to tree gathering fruit. Sometimes, those that lived close to the coastline soared for hours on the ocean breezes, dipping down to snatch fish from the water –" his speech grew more rapid, more animated "– and they clung to the cliff faces and the trees and the females flapped their wings and emitted their pheromones...their intoxicating musk ...

"...drivingpotentialmatescrazythemalesfoughtoverthewomenintheairandplummetedtotheirdeathstilldruggedfrenziedbythemuskanduuuuuhhhhh!"

Dolor tried to scramble up onto the table, up onto the cylinder, but the KeeZee O'lz had been ready for this. Quickly passing her gun to Ginko, she seized the man from behind in a bear hug and pulled him backwards, held him tightly as he squirmed and kicked his legs in the air. He let out a long, howling cry of frustrated lust. Dolor had had the hair on his head and eyebrows removed and replaced with silvery metal bristles, so these scraped at O'lz through her black jumpsuit, but it didn't faze her. She backed off further, and Ginko set aside the assault engine, went to the table, and turned off the two fans inside the cylinder. Its cover hissed back into place.

Gradually, after a drawn-out and violent shudder of spontaneous orgasm, Dolor went limp in O'lz's arms. Gently, like a mother who had calmed her child's tantrum, she set him down on his feet and released him.

He tottered a little but caught himself, looking down self-consciously at his still tented trousers. He had never experienced a climax of such intensity.

Still panting, Mr. Dolor looked up at Ginko with a semblance of his former professional demeanor and said, "I'll take it."

2: Valentin

Marcel Valentin had been a popular vid actor in Punktown for decades, and actors of his level of fame acquired a kind of immortality, but in his personal life he had endeavored to make that immortality a more literal thing. He was one-hundred-and-nine years old. Twenty-five years ago, when surgical procedures and an increasing measure of cybernetics had no longer been able to convincingly keep age at bay (more so on the inside than the outside), he had had himself cloned and his recorded memories transferred into this new body. His new body had been progressed only to the age of forty-two, when his flame had burned its brightest, and his original body had been incinerated. This procedure had been accomplished for him by the Neptune Teeb crime syndy, because cloning of private citizens (as opposed to clones used for labor and the military) was illegal.

But early this year, when his forty-two-year-old body had reached the age of sixty-seven, he had decided to have himself cloned a second time. He had this new vehicle for his memories advanced only to the age of twenty-nine, the age he had been when his star had first risen. The former clone was scrubbed of its memories (he couldn't share his life with another *him*, could he?) but he kept it around – in cryogenic storage at his vacation home down south in the Outback Colony – in case he ever wanted to produce a dead version of himself later, and go on with his life under a new identity. After all, at one-hundred-and-nine years-old, he had to reluctantly admit his long vid career was at an end. Short of computer trickery, how could he explain away his youthfulness in the public eye now, but to admit to illegal activities?

Ah, but it was a bittersweet thing, an aching tease, to be so young and handsome again, and yet not be able to play the rugged leading men, the tough-guy forcers, the violent gangsters he had specialized in. (Neptune Teeb himself had told Valentin he was a big fan.)

He tried to take his mind off this yearning for the past by indulging in activities that, within his Beaumonde Square penthouse, were shielded from the public eye. But a man of his wealth and long years had partaken of many varieties of pleasure. It could be a challenge devising or discovering more. That was one of the tasks he entrusted to his combination personal assistant, manservant, and bodyguard, Mr. Dolor.

Not that Mr. Dolor was his only servant. Recently he had hired a Sinanese woman as his housecleaner. He had had a couple of Sinanese lovers before; one a woman, one a ladyboy. Both had been beautiful. Like all Sinanese, who hailed from the world Sinan in a coexistent dimension, his housekeeper Lhi was on the short side, with long black hair and pale blue skin. She was in her late twenties, he figured, and a little meatier than his past lovers, but still sufficiently attractive. Only a week into her employment, he had cornered her one day in the guest bedroom while she was cleaning and pressed himself upon her. She had given in, after initial inarticulate protests (her English was limited) and a few tears, and he had tucked a hundred munit bill into her hand afterwards, stroking that long hair soothingly and encouraging her to go buy herself something nice when it was time to go home.

A Sinanese man, also with limited English skills, picked her up in a hovercar at street level every evening. Lhi had told Valentin once the man was her sister. Valentin had laughed. Lhi and her cutely skewed (if occasionally exasperating) English.

Now, whenever he was hungry and he was too lazy to have Dolor summon here a professional working girl or boy – human, otherworlder, or mutant – he simply took Lhi again. Their second time, she had held her hand out to him afterwards, and held him with a stern gaze. *Ah, the mercenary little bitch!* he thought. But he always gave her the hundred munits, presumably to share with her "sister."

Lhi was presently down in the kitchen, tidying up after dinner, soon to finish for the evening. Valentin and Mr. Dolor were down the hall in the penthouse's playroom. Dolor had just finished setting up the item he had acquired that morning. The "fairy," as it had been called.

The cylinder stood against one wall, tilted but held in place by a frame Dolor had improvised, the capsule's lid still in place. Opposite this silvery coffin was the playroom's bed, its mattress fitted with a sheet of bioengineered living human skin. The bed already had wrist and ankle restraints.

Valentin was not self-conscious about disrobing in front of Mr. Dolor. Mr. Dolor had seen it all. When Valentin had stretched out on his back on the bed and extended his extremities to its four corners, Dolor secured the restraints. Along with the fairy in its receptacle, Osman Ginko had given Dolor the two gas masks. Unlike his first encounter with the mummified Fahleet, Dolor was wearing one of those masks now.

"Butterflies and zebras and moonbeams," Valentin said, smiling, as he watched Dolor strap his left ankle. His again-youthful manhood was already stirring from its sleep. "Is that what I'm going to see, Mr. Dolor?"

"Excuse me, sir?" The gas mask with its blank lenses for eyes lifted quizzically.

"Nothing."

When Valentin was pinned in place, his body a muscular white X, Dolor turned to the cylinder. He touched a key on its side, and its cover slid aside with a whisper.

Valentin strained to lift his head to look upon his acquisition. "Jee-sus," he said, "is that thing hideous." But in anticipation of the fairy's arrival, he had watched old vids of the Fahleet in life, copulating in trees, the females clinging to rough bark while the males mounted them. In life, the nude little beings with their odd gliding webs had been decidedly more enticing.

Dolor pressed a second key, and then stood aside, as fans within the cylinder blew toward Valentin an unseen, microscopic pollen...not made less potent by the being's decay, but perhaps even fermented to a greater headiness. Tiny motes of the Fahleet itself were borne along, entering Valentin's body through his nostrils and greedily gulping mouth.

"Ohhh, *man*," he said, his head still lifted from the living skin of the bed as he kept his eyes trained on the fairy's own half-closed/half-opened black eyes. "Did you see this, Mr. Dolor?"

"Tell me what you see, sir," said Dolor with his glinting metal hair.

"I can see them! It's like I'm looking through the eyes of one of them! I'm flying, man...I'm *flying*." He laughed drunkenly, astonished, delighted. "I'm flying over the ocean, Mr. Dolor – I can see my shadow below me on the water! Oh my God...I'm following a smell...an incredible, heavenly scent. A heaven-sent scent!" He laughed again, wildly.

Wheeling on high, soaring like a kite on the ocean updrafts, Valentin looked toward a wall of rugged white cliffs and spotted the source of the intoxicating aroma. A female, clinging to the chalky rock and flapping her gliding membranes with languorous, sensuous movements. Somehow, he knew, it was *this* female...the one in this very room with him.

Valentin swooped down toward her...closer...closer...alighted upon her back. In this vision, this memory, he penetrated her and she threw back her long pointed head and let out a ululating cry of pleasure.

Valentin jerked his wrists against their bonds. Tendons showed hard in his neck. "Mr. Dolor!" he rasped through gritted teeth. "Oh God, Mr. Dolor...unstrap me! Hurry!"

"Sir," Dolor said calmly through his muffling mask. "Remember, you yourself told me not to allow you to damage the fairy."

"I need her! *I need her!*"

"I'm sorry, sir, I must follow your orders."

Valentin turned on his assistant a look of rage that even the most bloodthirsty gangster he had ever portrayed, the most righteous forcer vowing vengeance over the body of his slain partner, had never evinced. "Go get me that girl downstairs – quickly!"

"Lhi?"

"Who the blast do you think I mean?" Valentin screeched. "Give her five hundred munits, if you have to, but get her up here!"

Dolor left the room, and though Valentin squeezed his eyes tightly shut to hold off from climaxing before his assistant could return with his housekeeper, it did nothing to cut off the ancient memories he relived as the pair of Fahleets – vainly, as it turned out – strove amorously to perpetuate their species.

Only a minute later, however, Dolor returned, holding a confused looking Lhi by the arm. Her eyes widened at the sight of her employer naked upon the playroom bed.

Valentin opened his eyes, saw her there, and grinned...his great rictus, trembling like a drawn bow, rather like that on the mummy's own face. To Dolor, he said, "Now unstrap me." Then, to Lhi, he instructed, "Take a deep breath, sweetness."

3: Yue

Having brought his secondhand hovercar alongside the curb in front of the looming Beaumonde Square apartment tower, Yue opened the passenger's side door when he saw his sister emerging from the building's revolving front door. It wasn't until she bent down and slipped in beside him, however, that he noticed her disheveled hair, hanging across her face, the suction bruises spotting her throat, the tears capping her eyes.

In their native Sinanese tongue, he snarled, "What did he do to you?"

Lhi had never dared tell her brother about how her employer had seduced her. She had told Yue the bonus money she shared with him was tips for her conventional work. This time, though, with the last of her monumental orgasm still echoing through the channels of her body – a tremor she felt sure he could sense – and the smell of sex strong in this enclosed space, she knew she could no longer deceive him. All she could say, in a small gasping voice, was, "Please take me home."

"Did he dishonor you, sister?" Yue demanded.

"Please, Yue...take me home."

Yue looked at her, hard. In certain light, the black Sinanese eye seemed to reflect a red light. His eyes flashed red now. Yue had done bad things in order to bring his sister to what he had hoped would be a better life in this dimension, on this world Oasis, in this city originally called Paxton, created by Earth colonists generations ago. He had sacrificed, he had compromised his integrity, he had even killed (unbeknownst to her) for his younger sister's sake.

He looked through the windshield, no longer pressing her, and started the car forward again. But he circled around to the entrance to the tower's subterranean parking lot.

"Please, Yue, don't," his sister pleaded.

His jaw thrust forward, his body filled with a vibration like but unlike the vibration that shimmered in Lhi's body, he disregarded her pleas, until finally she lapsed into respectful, fatalistic silence.

Though she was an independent worker, not one of the building's official cleaning staff, Valentin had arranged for Lhi to have access to the service elevator at the rear of the building. She and her brother rode in this now, up to the top of the building. During this ascent, Yue continuously muttered the worst of profanity and curses under his breath. For her part, Lhi kept her eyes downcast and fought the urge to vomit.

They walked to the door of Marcel Valentin's penthouse apartment, and Lhi whispered one last time, "Please." Yue ignored her and rang the buzzer.

In the door's vidplate appeared the head of Mr. Dolor, topped with its sparkling metal bristles. "Oh, hello, Lhi. Did you forget something?"

"She forgot pocketbook," Yue said tersely.

They heard the hard clack of the door unbolting, and then it slid open with a hiss.

Yue had a handgun, held down by his thigh. It was not unusual that he owned a handgun; this was Punktown. Yue also had the instincts of a fighter, and knew that Mr. Dolor was not someone to point a gun at to threaten and question. Mr. Dolor would no doubt have a gun of his own. Mr. Dolor would doubtlessly have done his own bad things; it was his job to do bad things. So, Yue pointed the gun at him and simply pulled the trigger.

Yue shot Mr. Dolor in the cheek and jaw and neck and Lhi cried out and squeezed her eyes shut, but as Mr. Dolor fell back to splay on the floor with his limbs flung out in an X, Yue dragged his sister into the apartment and hit the button to close the door behind them.

"What the hell was that?" they heard a voice call from deeper in the apartment. "Mr. Dolor? *Mr. Dolor?*"

"Call to him!" Yue hissed to his sister.

"Yue!"

"*Do it!*"

"Mr. Valentin?" Lhi called out. "It is Lhi!"

Around the corner of a doorway, Marcel Valentin leaned his upper body out and said, "Lhi? What were those sounds?" And then he saw Yue take a step forward, once more lifting his pistol. Valentin ducked back with a shriek that none of the tough forcers and gangsters he had played would ever have uttered. Two shots from Yue's pistol chewed into the doorframe, and then Yue broke into a run and lunged through the threshold.

At the end of a long hallway lined with holographic movie posters he saw Valentin, dressed in a beautifully embroidered silk Ramon robe, about to duck through another doorway. Yue fired two more shots. He heard Valentin scream again shrilly, and the man slammed up against the wall at the hallway's terminus, but he still managed to plunge awkwardly through the open doorway. For his part, Yue was reluctant to exhaust his gun's ammo until he was closer, his target more assured.

"What you do my sister, you fuck?" he shouted, stalking down the hallway with Lhi scrunched down behind him. "Huh? You disgrace my sister like animal?"

Just a few steps before Yue reached the doorway, a more expensive gun than his own was thrust out and Valentin blindly fired several short, red streaks of energy instead of solid bullets. They left smoking black holes in the hallway's left-hand wall, but struck neither of the Sinanese siblings.

Yue ducked down a bit, mindful to keep Lhi shielded behind him, and blasted off three more rounds into the room beyond. He heard a kind of *oomph*, then the thump of a heavy object striking the floor.

Cautiously, Yue leaned closer to peek into the room, ready to fire his last rounds. He saw it wasn't necessary. Though somewhere down south, unknown to anyone alive, an older version of the actor Marcel Valentin lay mindlessly alive in a stasis chamber, this incarnation of him was dead, with two holes drilled into the V of chest exposed by his robe. He had learned little, it would seem, from the countless gun battles he had participated in during his vids.

The floor upon which he lay was that of the playroom, dominated by the bed with its sheet of living skin and its restraining straps...and facing that, leaning in a kind of support frame, an odd metal capsule large enough to contain a child.

"The thing is in that," Lhi said, pointing.

"What thing?" Yue asked.

"The body of a dead person...or animal...I don't know. Not an Earther, not Sinanese. It has wings, and it has some kind of magic that takes over your mind with visions."

Yue took a step toward the metal cylinder but Lhi cried, "No!" Grabbed onto his arm. She didn't want to tell him how terrible that magic was. That if he opened the cylinder, released the spell bottled up inside, Yue would disgrace his sister himself...and she would *enjoy* it. She could never tell him how she had enjoyed what Valentin had done to her, enjoyed it beyond any physical experience she had ever known.

"Did this monster kill the person inside?"

"No...it has been dead for many years."

Yue looked at the bed, the straps, then at his sister. He didn't want to ask her to confirm what he envisioned. Instead he said, "We should take this poor being and remove it from here, to be buried properly or burned, so no one like that decadent fiend will abuse its magic again."

"But we mustn't open it, ever!" Lhi implored.

"We won't take any money, any of his valuables," Yue mused aloud, glancing around him. "I don't want to poison my future, and damn my soul. But this relic is coming with us."

Tucking his gun into his rear waistband, Yue went to the cylinder and lifted it into his arms. He had thought he might need his sister to help him carry it, but the metal was light and so, apparently, were the capsule's contents.

Lhi preceded him back the way they had come, careful to keep her eyes off the body of Mr. Dolor, in its growing pool of blood, on their way to the door.

They rode the service elevator down to the underground parking lot, and Yue placed the cylinder in the trunk of his hovercar.

"The forcers will be looking for us, I'm sure of it," Lhi fretted as she climbed back into the passenger's seat. "I'm sure there are security vids they will look at."

"Let the forcers look for us," Yue said, starting up the vehicle, causing it to rise several feet into the air. "Forcers have looked for me before, here and back home. This city is big. We are unimportant in its eyes. We will disappear." He blew across his upturned palm, as if to disperse some unseen dust.

4: Mhin

Some months back Yue and Lhi had rented an apartment on the third floor of a small brick building of pre-colonial Choom origin – the Choom being the native people of Oasis – on Forma Street. The ground floor was occupied by an apothecary run by Yue's friend, and landlord, Mhin. Mhin was thickly built and big-bellied for a Sinanese, but on their world this was a matter of pride; it indicated one was well-fed, and hence comfortable financially. He had lost an eye and scarred half his face in an explosion back on Sinan, while mixing a volatile potion, and now wore a tubular optical device in that socket which gave him enhanced vision almost on the level of the tendril-eyed Tikkihotto race.

Yue had sent Lhi upstairs to hurriedly pack what she needed to bring with them, while Yue and Mhin talked in the latter's workshop at the rear of his store. Without getting into his sister's humiliation, Yue explained to his friend that they were in trouble and had to pull up roots fast.

"Brother," Yue said in their language, "it shames me to ask you, but can you lend me some money? A thousand munits, maybe? You know I'll repay you when I can." He didn't mention the five hundred munits he already had on him. Lhi had pushed the bills into his hand before they'd left the car, without being able to meet her brother's eyes.

"Can't you tell me what is wrong?" Mhin asked.

"It has to do with Lhi's employer. The vid star. You'll see it on the news. And I took something from him, that I would like to dispose of properly. The body of some strange being, Lhi tells me, with magical properties. I don't want to be caught with it, and I would hate to bury it in some filthy abandoned lot in this city, but I don't want to just throw it into a trash zapper. Do you have anything like an incinerator in the basement?"

"Only the trash zapper out back. You say magical properties? How so?" Mhin, less superstitious than his friend, did not believe in magic, despite the potions he sold in his shop. He considered himself a scientist.

"She said breathing in the atmosphere of this being infects the mind...brings visions. It's a small mummy of some kind, with wings."

"Where is it now?"

"In a container, in the trunk of my car."

"Bring it to me."

"Aren't you afraid to be infected?"

From a hook on the wall beside him, Mhin took down a mask he wore when mixing chemicals and ingredients that were best not inhaled freely. "I'll take precautions."

Yue carried the cylinder into the shop through its back entrance, out of the view of Forma Street's traffic and pedestrians, and laid it on Mhin's work table. Mhin told Yue to go upstairs and help Lhi pack while he examined the capsule's occupant.

Alone, Mhin easily found the means by which to open the little coffin's cover, and when confronted by the withered entity inside he said, "Well...and just who are you, old thing?"

He took a picture of the diminutive gray figure with his wrist comp, then ran a query on the net. He came up with a result immediately...and he read about the race called the Fahleet, long exterminated by the predominant race on Kali.

He read of the pheromones the females emitted to attract males during the season of mating, when males would be so driven to a frenzy that they might battle to the death over the object of their desire. But this shriveled corpse, its juices all drained, still emanated these compounds?

Mhin used a scalpel to scrape some dry flakes of skin from one of the mummy's wing-like gliding membranes, and deposited the sample into a scanner. He pored over the results, rubbing his chin with a gloved hand. Turning back to face the body, he studied its face through various different filters and magnifications of his optical device. Under one such filter, its half-lidded obsidian eyes seems to twinkle at him with myriad restless light specks, a constellation of twitching stars not fixed right in the firmament, and he shuddered. As if some mysterious vestige of life still imbued this creature. Who could say? Maybe magic was just science he hadn't yet encountered.

When Yue came back downstairs and cautiously poked his head into the workshop, to find Mhin had sealed the container again, Mhin gestured for him to enter and said, "You had better get as far from this neighborhood as you can. Maybe even leave the city, go to Miniosis or the Outback Colony, if you can. Here." He produced an unlocked cash box, and from it counted out three thousand munits in bills. He handed these to the other blue-skinned man. "This is not a loan. Take your sister away from here."

Yue wagged his head in awe, staring at the bills, then shoved them into his pocket and said, "I am forever in your debt, brother."

"Listen, don't worry about this thing." He motioned toward the cylinder behind him. "I'll deal with it."

"You will? Thank you, Mhin. But please...don't just toss it into a zapper where trash is burned. Or, if you have no choice, at least say some prayers over it."

"I promise, I will say prayers," Mhin said. "Don't worry...I'll dispose of the body."

It was not entirely a lie.

5: Ginko

There had been no security cameras in the home of Marcel Valentin. Osman Ginko imagined the actor had wanted no record of his activities to be blackmailed with. There had, though, been security cameras in the halls of the building which housed Valentin's penthouse, and they showed a Sinanese woman who had been in his employ leaving his apartment in the company of a Sinanese man who may have been her husband or boyfriend, this man carrying a metal cylinder in his arms. What the cylinder had contained, however, the forcers did not know. An inventory of Valentin's belongings was still being assembled, a difficult process with his assistant having been murdered along with him.

Ginko had his fingers on the pulse of Punktown, so he could gauge its desires, its needs. He was familiar with neighborhoods dominated by this or that race of otherworlders, where rare and exotic curiosities could be found.

He had been to the Sinanese apothecary on Forma Street numerous times in the past. He knew the proprietor by name. Mhin was not alarmed to see Ginko step through the front door of his shop in the presence of the towering albino KeeZee female. "Ah, my friends!" he exclaimed. "Would you care for some tea?"

"Please, Mhin – thank you," said Ginko.

Ginko's gaze roved over the shelves all around him, their surfaces crammed full with tiny labeled bottles and sealed baggies. These held powders of every color and consistency, derived from minerals and plants and animals, often in combination. Some jars contained loose leaves and twigs, insects, the dehydrated bodies of tiny lizards. Preserved in jars of fluid were larval benders. A creature native to Sinan, an adult bender would present itself as a jellyfish as large as a parachute, drifting upon air currents, the dangling tendrils of which delivered a poison that – if it didn't prove fatal – was said to bring on precognitive visions.

Mhin came back with their tea, and the three of them sat at a small table off to one side, while a younger Sinanese man took over at the counter to tend to an old Choom woman seeking some medicinal herbs.

"What can I do for you today, my friend?" Mhin asked.

"I'm helping a client of mine, an important businessman, prepare for a grand party at his home," Ginko explained. "He seeks entertainments of a novel character."

"Your specialty, of course!"

Taking in both men with her three pink eyes, O'lz extended a clear tubular tongue from between her bony, fang-filled jaws and used it to suck at her tea.

"Substances," Ginko went on, "with unique properties he may not have experienced before."

Mhin swept his arm toward the shelf containing jars of pickled benders. "Then might I recommend?"

"Perhaps, perhaps, but I had another thing in mind, specifically. Have your ever come into possession of the body of a race called the Fahleet? They are extinct, now, but were originally to be found on Kali."

Ginko could tell from the way the Sinanese man's face tightened up and his one eye turned wary that his instincts had been correct. "A race called...?"

"My friend," Ginko said in a lower voice, hunching forward, "you know me. I'm not an informer for the forcers. Word on the street –"

"There can't have been any word on the street. Not yet."

"My intuition, then, is that you possess a body. I'd like to purchase it from you."

"I have no body of a Fahleet," Mhin replied. He hesitated, but Ginko saw the hesitation pass. After all, they had done business many times, and the very point of coming into possession of unique materials was to provide them to his customers. He continued, "What I have, however, is the powdered essence of a Fahleet."

"I see," said Ginko, only somewhat disappointed. He would not ask the man how he had come by this substance; it wasn't actually important now that it was established he was in possession of it. "And it serves as a potent aphrodisiac, as I understand?"

"*Most* effective," Mhin said solemnly.

"And how does one administer this essence?"

"I would recommend sniffing a mere pinch from the palm, or snorting a line of it from a mirror."

"And have you tried this substance yourself?"

The ever observant Osman Ginko noted that Mhin couldn't prevent himself from glancing guiltily at the young male assistant who at that moment was giving the old Choom woman her change. "I have sampled it. It is an aphrodisiac like no other."

"I think this is exactly the kind of thing my client would be interested in," Ginko said.

"Then I'll show you."

Mhin took Ginko and O'lz to his workshop in the back of the store, and here he bent down to pull out a large drawer from a wall into which were set rows and rows of labeled drawers. "How many jars of this essence might you desire?" Mhin asked. "I'll caution you that the material is very concentrated, very powerful in small doses."

Ginko stepped closer to look down into the drawer, at two dozen small bottles into which were dispersed the crushed and powdered remnants of a long-dead fairy.

"Just one jar today, my friend, now that I know you have this," said Osman Ginko, reaching for his wallet.

But he was certain he would be back for more in the future. Punktown was, after all, a city of ceaseless and prodigious appetite.

ABOUT THE AUTHOR

Jeffrey Thomas is an American author of weird fiction, the creator of the acclaimed setting Punktown. Books in the Punktown universe include the short story collections PUNKTOWN, VOICES FROM PUNKTOWN, PUNKTOWN: SHADES OF GREY (with his brother, Scott Thomas), GHOSTS OF PUNKTOWN, and the shared world anthology TRANSMISSIONS FROM PUNKTOWN. Novels in that setting include DEADSTOCK, BLUE WAR, MONSTROCITY, HEALTH AGENT, EVERYBODY SCREAM!, and RED CELLS. Thomas's other short story collections include THE ENDLESS FALL, HAUNTED WORLDS, WORSHIP THE NIGHT, THIRTEEN SPECIMENS, NOCTURNAL EMISSIONS, DOOMSDAYS, TERROR INCOGNITA, UNHOLY DIMENSIONS, AAAIIIEEE!!!, HONEY IS SWEETER THAN BLOOD, and ENCOUNTERS WITH ENOCH COFFIN (with W. H. Pugmire). His other novels include LETTERS FROM HADES, THE FALL OF HADES, BEAUTIFUL HELL, BONELAND, BEYOND THE DOOR, THOUGHT FORMS, SUBJECT 11, LOST IN DARKNESS, THE SEA OF FLESH AND ASH (with his brother, Scott Thomas), BLOOD SOCIETY, and A NIGHTMARE ON ELM STREET: THE DREAM DEALERS. Thomas lives in Massachusetts.

Visit the author on Facebook at:
https://www.facebook.com/jeffrey.thomas.71

Also in the Jeffrey Thomas Chapbook Series:
#1 THE COMING OF THE OLD ONES:
A Trio of Lovecraftian Stories

Made in the USA
Middletown, DE
12 June 2021